This book belongs to: **Father Christmas**

Address: **The Clouds**

GULLANE
CHILDREN'S BOOKS

This book contains:

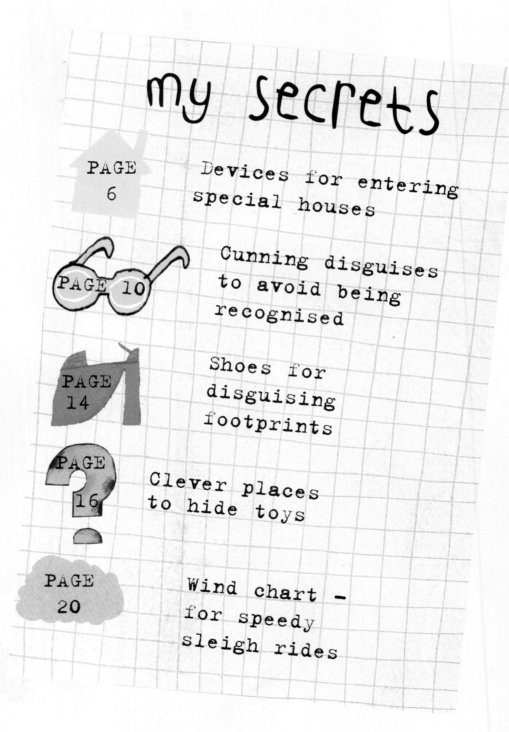

my secrets

private things

my diary

my projects

Devices for entering special houses

cave*

*This bear mask
is very handy
for making friends
during risky deliveries.

Hindu palace

Kennel

Very important:

1. Don't let reindeer into the house (they make a mess).

2. Don't turn on the lights.

3. Don't take anything from the fridge, however delicious it looks.

Cunning disguises to avoid being recognised

1. Swan

Make sure I don't fall off the roof!

2. Tree

Problem! Difficult to get up without help!

3. Teddy bear

Be careful: beard can get stuck in zip!

4. Building blocks

5. Road sweeper

Try not to get beard caught in broom.

6. Ghost

Problem: scary for children.

7. Rapper

Very cool disguise.
The elves' favourite.

Dance moves.

8. Tourist

Watch out for crabs and sunburn!

9. Bullfighter

Bad idea: the colour red excites the reindeer.

10. Computer

Make sure I don't get trapped inside!

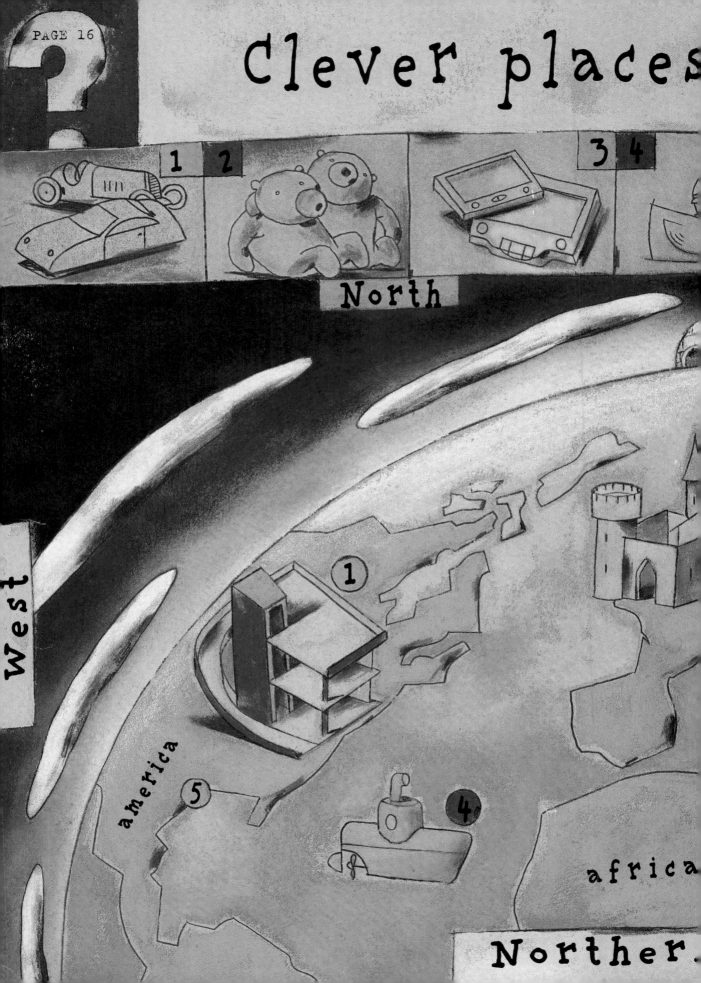

Clever places

1 2 3 4

North

West

1

america

5

4

africa

Norther.

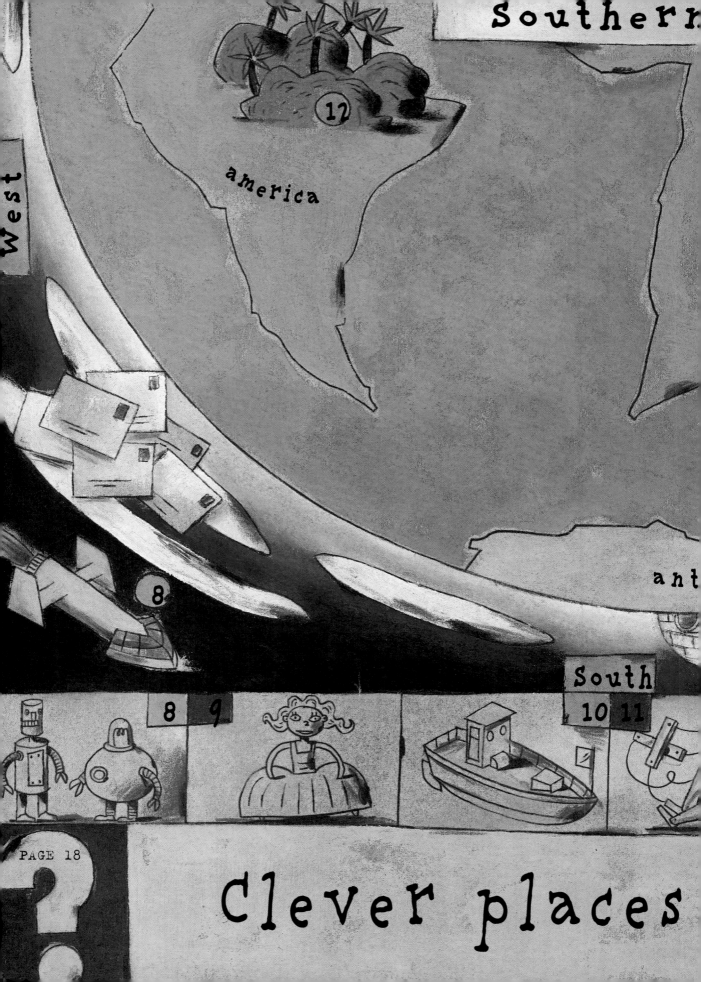

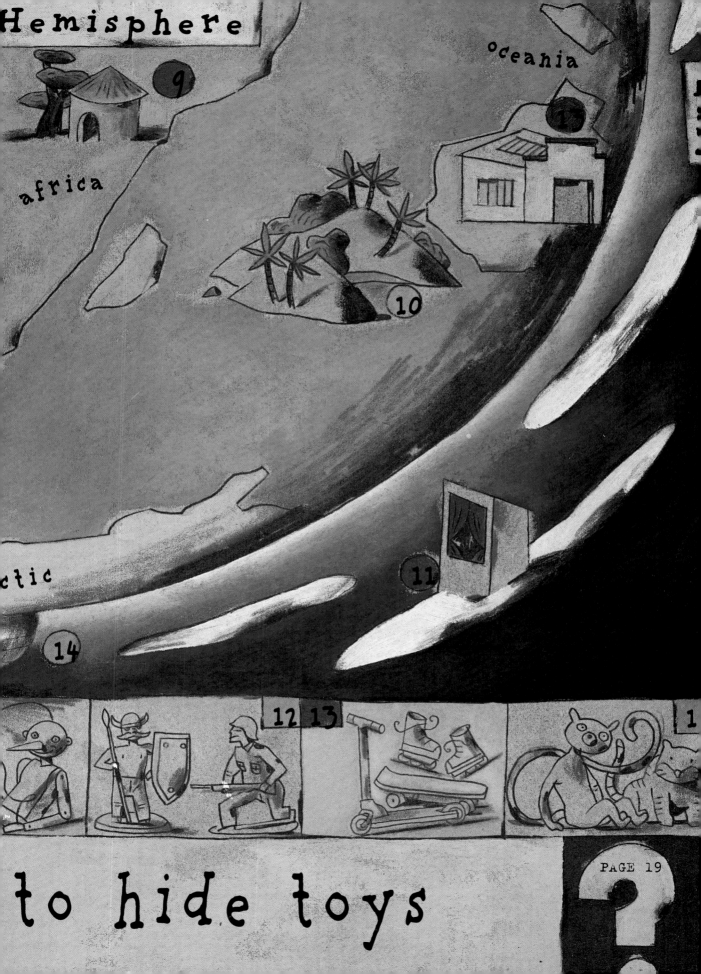

Wind chart

Cold wind: brr! Button up my coat.

NORTH POLE

North wind:
strong and icy.
Put on my hat
and tighten
my seat belt!

for speedy sleigh rides

Breeze:
little light wind.

Warm, dry wind:
unbutton my coat.

My favourite pictures

Me, at the start of my career.

Me waking up, photographed by Billy, my reindeer.

Me, trying to get down the chimney (very tricky).

Me, on Christmas Eve.

Me, on Christmas morning.

Luckily, Billy is always
there to help me!

Me, clean-shaven
and suntanned.

Party time for the elves.

My friend Little Mouse's birthday.

Billy, Bo,
Thorwald and Linus,
my reindeer.

Snowball fight!

Billy and me,
messing around

Badminton match against
Rumpelstiltskin. (I WIN!)

Me, the day
I was recognised!

sloppy kisses
for Father
Christmas

Snow White

The photo Snow White sent me.

Portraits of me

Me, painted by Leonardo da Vinci.

Me, painted by Auguste Renoir.

Me, painted by Pablo Picasso.

Me, painted by Andy Warhol.

Important letters

Father Christmas,

You didn't eat the plate of ravioli I left by the fireplace especially for you. So now I am sending it by post. I hope it doesn't get too messy.

Joseph age 5

FATHER CHRISTMAS

PLEASE COME AND STAY AT MY HOUSE FROM 26TH MARCH TILL 3RD APRIL. MY BROTHER WON'T BE THERE SO YOU CAN SLEEP IN HIS BED.

YOU DON'T NEED TO BRING ANY PRESENTS, BUT IF YOU HAPPEN TO HAVE ANY, THAT'S OKAY.

bed

OSCAR AGE 7

reindeer fur →

Dear Father Christmas,
I want a dog for Christmas.
I asked for one last year
but you brought me a little
brother instead.
I'm not complaining, because
he's quite cute.
But this year, don't mess
about, Father Christmas.
buy me a dog — or watch
out!

Father christmas
in the sky

☎ 0178323569126724

23
16
+ 16
55

Dear Father Christmas,
My name is Barnaby the teddy bear.
You gave me to a little girl. She is
very sweet. But her dolls keep
dressing me up in jewels. Can
you please tell them to stop?

Barnaby
— X —

FATHER CHRISTMAS

I AM NOT HAPPY! I ORDERED
THREE CHILDREN LAST YEAR AND
DIDN'T GET ANY! MAYBE YOU JUST
FORGOT, FATHER CHRISTMAS? I
HOPE YOU WON'T FORGET THIS YEAR.
AND I HOPE YOU'LL BRING ME AN
EXTRA CHILD TO MAKE UP FOR IT.

BIG FEET, THE OGRE

wrapping
paper
designs

Santa Claus
I am an old puppet. I got thrown away with
the rubbish, but I'm sure I could make somebody
happy. You just need to come and find me
and smarten me up a bit.

I'm waiting.

Punch, age 68

SKY POLICE

OFFENCE: Ignoring the speed limit

FOR: Mr. Christmas

ADDRESS: Unknown

Chief of SKY POLICE: Chief

Mr Claus

To go with your red coat, we recommend a range of undergarments:

Vest

Socks

Warm leggings for cold nights

Night Cap

NEW! Undergarments for reindeer

TRIAL COUPON
Satisfaction guaranteed or your money back

DEAR
FATHER
CHRISTMAS

I AM THE FASTEST REINDEER IN THE UNIVERSE. IF YOU LIKE, I CAN PULL YOUR SLEIGH. BUT YOU BETTER FASTEN YOUR SEATBELT !

My Big Scrumptious Popsicle,

I was on my broom when I saw you go past on your sleigh. My you looked handsome? Why dont you drop by for a nice cup of fly-wing tea and some kisses and cuddles.

Glugba the Witch
X X

$1 \times 2 = 2$
$2 \times 2 = 4$
$3 \times 2 = 6$
$4 \times 2 = 8$
$5 \times 2 = 10$
$6 \times 2 = 12$
$7 \times 2 = 14$
$8 \times 2 = 16$

my diary

JANUARY

Notes from January

Each year, after I've delivered all my presents, I am SO tired I just stay in bed for the whole month.

I only get up to make myself another cup of hot chocolate. And when I get back to bed, who do I find tucked up under the duvet?

My reindeer!

I move them to one side, and get back into bed. I grab my teddy, I close my eyes, and I've nearly drifted off... when the reindeer start to snore! I put my head under the pillow, I hug my teddy, I'm almost asleep again... And then, guess what? One reindeer turns over, another pulls the duvet off, a third one sneezes... Well by now I've had enough.
I jump out of bed and chase them all away.

Enough!

I get back into bed, I cuddle my teddy, I go back to sleep... and once again the duvet moves! I open one eye: now the elves are climbing into my bed!
I let out a huge sigh.

The sneaky reindeer seize the chance to come back... I'm about to lose my temper big time, when they start to sing a soothing lullaby:

♫

– Hush a bye Santa
Tucked up in bed,
Go back to sleep now,
Rest your old head.

Well, how can I help but fall well and truly asleep?

Snore Zzzzz Snore zzzzz...

FEBRUARY

f 1
S 2
S 3

Wake up
(well, try to).

m 4
t 5
w 6
t 7
f 8
S 9
S 10

Fill the cloud
with stuffing.

m 11
t 12
w 13
t 14
f 15
S 16
S 17

m 18
t 19
w 20
t 21
f 22
S 23
S 24

Re-paint the
cloud (white).

m 25
t 26
w 27
t 28

Big tidy-up.

Notes from February

– Get up,
Father Christmas,
get up!
IT'S FEBRUARY!!!

The reindeer and the elves are awake. They try to get me out of bed, but I'm too tired to open my eyes. The reindeer pull the duvet off. The elves draw back the curtains. I hold onto my teddy and I keep my eyes firmly closed.

The elves run to fetch their musical instruments.
A fanfare plays three centimetres from my ear but
I refuse to wake up.

The reindeer start to sing.

The bed begins to shake.

The planets move to the rhythm of the music, but I
don't hear a thing. I sleep, hugging my teddy tight.

This goes on for hours, days...
Then all of a sudden the noise stops. I open one eye:
the reindeer, the elves, the clouds, the planets,
the whole world has gone back to sleep.

So, without making a sound, I get up,
tiptoe to the kitchen, and make myself

an enormous,

gigantic,

monstrous

breakfast!

MARCH

f 1 Shape my cloud into a flower.
S 2
S 3

m 4
t 5
w 6
t 7
f 8 Make chips.
S 9
S 10

m 11
t 12 Start lessons with reindeer and elves.
w 13
t 14
f 15
S 16
S 17

m 18
t 19 spring!
w 20
t 21
f 22
S 23
S 24

m 25 Invent some new games.
t 26
w 27
t 28
f 29
S 30
S 31 Do the washing!

In March, at elf school, we have writing lessons ...

bake cakes ...

do some drawing ... and have fun!

Notes from March

One morning I make myself a cup of hot chocolate,
I butter my toast and I rush to collect the post. I love to
read my letters while I eat breakfast. But when I open
my letterbox, it's empty!

All of a sudden I feel so sad that I think I'm
about to cry.

Attracted by the smell of chocolate, Billy, my favourite reindeer arrives, yawning sleepily:

– You look unhappy, my old Pops.

I reply sulkily:

– I haven't had a single thankyou letter. I bring presents to all those children, and not one of them writes to say thank you.

Billy sits down and puts his arm around me.
– Now listen, Pops, the children play with the toys you bring them. They're happy. And their happiness is their way of thanking you.
– You're right, I say.

My reindeer gives me a kiss on the cheek. It scratches a bit, but I feel much better.

– Pops, Billy says then, if you give me a piece of toast
and jam, I will write you a thankyou letter straightaway.
– No need to do that, I say, spreading jam on the toast.
Your happiness is enough for me.

Then that cheeky Billy ties a napkin round his neck, and
with a
sly little smile,
he starts to eat his delicious toast.

APRIL

m 1
t 2   Shape my cloud into a fish.
w 3
t 4
f 5
S 6
S 7

m 15
t 16   Mission to Earth.
w 17
t 18
f 19
S 20
S 21

m 8   Remember to buy toothbrush for my mission to Earth.
t 9
w 10
t 11
f 12
S 13   Spring holidays for elves.
S 14

m 22
t 23
w 24
t 25
f 26
S 27   Back from mission to Earth.
S 28

WHAT A SMILE!

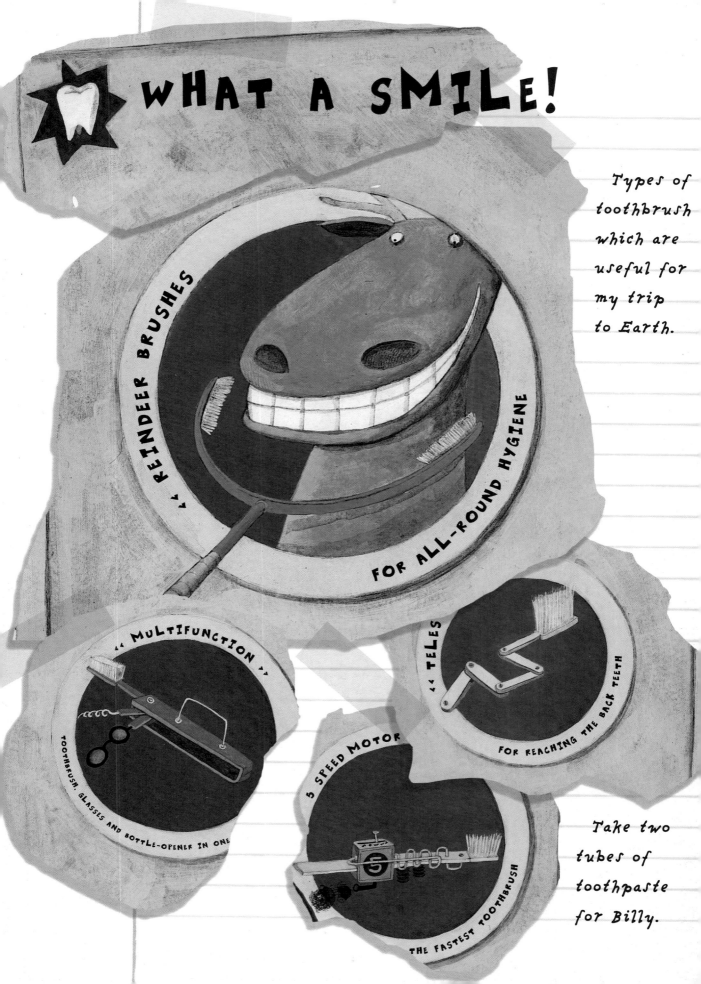

Types of toothbrush which are useful for my trip to Earth.

"REINDEER BRUSHES" FOR ALL-ROUND HYGIENE

"MULTIFUNCTION"

TOOTHBRUSH, GLASSES AND BOTTLE-OPENER IN ONE

"TELES

FOR REACHING THE BACK TEETH

5 SPEED MOTOR

THE FASTEST TOOTHBRUSH

Take two tubes of toothpaste for Billy.

Notes from April

At this time of year I pay a visit to Earth with my reindeer, Billy. I need to find out what toys the children are playing with, but I must not be recognised. I put on a cunning disguise and . . .

I keep my eyes and ears open

On the last day of my mission, I walk past a cake shop. I pretend not to see it.
But I can't resist, I go in and I come out with:
croissants, danish pastries,
doughnuts,
muffins,
custard tarts,
meringues,
éclairs and
strawberry tarts...

I sit peacefully on a bench and one by one I eat the croissants, danish pastries, doughnuts, muffins, custard tarts, meringues, éclairs and strawberry tarts...

Then Billy arrives. He helps me to finish eating the cakes. When we are completely full, we head back to our cloud.

It's strange,
      but our journey home
           seems very, very slow.

MAY

w 1
t 2
f 3
S 4
S 5

My friend Little Mouse's birthday.

m 6
t 7
w 8
t 9
f 10
S 11
S 12

m 13
t 14
w 15

Elf school.

m 20
t 21
w 22
t 23
f 24
S 25
S 26

Make chocolate mousse.

sugar   saucepan

whisk

cream   chocolate

butter

m 27
t 28
w 29
t 30
f 31

Washday.

Magic tricks: one, two, three . . . Hey Presto!

Notes from May

One morning, who should I find on my cloud but a little girl attached to an enormous balloon. She calmly takes a banana out of her pocket, and points it at me.
- Hand over the toys, Father Christmas!
- Not on your life! I say, trembling. These are my toys.
- I order you! replies the little girl. So hurry up and give them to me, or else!

I pretend to look worried. But with my foot I press a lever which opens a secret trapdoor in the cloud. And whee! the little girl falls through and drifts downwards. I send Billy to fetch her and bring her back up.
— So, who is giving the orders? I joke.
— You, Father Christmas, she sobs.

I give her a handkerchief and ask her name.
— Zaza, she replies, wiping her eyes.

- And where do you live, Zaza?
- Nowhere, I am a poor little orphan.
  I raise my eyes to the sky, sighing,
- Oh dear dear! What am I to do with you now?
  I have a think, then I rummage about in my
  clothes trunk and pull out an elf suit.

- Put this on, little Zaza: I am giving you a job as an elf!
While you get changed, I will make you some hot chocolate.
  But before the milk is even heated up, the elves come to
      fetch their new little helper, and take her off
              to play on their cloud.

              And I drink the hot chocolate
                    down in one big gulp!

JUNE

S 1
S 2

Mend the leaks in the cloud.

m 3
t 4
w 5
t 6
f 7
S 8
S 9

Paella night with Gluglu the witch.

m 10
t 11
w 12

Elf school.

m 17
t 18
w 19
t 20
f 21
S 22
S 23

Think about buying sun cream, mask and snorkel.

m 24
t 25
w 26
t 27

Big end-of-school party.

Exercise, sing, dance: at elf school we go wild!

Shape my cloud into a hat.

Notes from June

    Because it is such a lovely day, I decide to go back down to Earth with Billy. We go for a walk in the woods. Wandering into a clearing, I spot a flower. In all my long life as Father Christmas, I have never seen such a pretty flower! I reach down to pick it.

– What are you doing? Billy cries.

I reply:

– I love this flower, I want to bring it back to my cloud.

– If you pick it, it will die, says Billy.

– I want it!

– Pops, you cannot do that!

I sit down. I sulk.

– Listen, says Billy softly, let's go home. You will have forgotten about it by tomorrow.

I say goodbye to the flower, jump on Billy's back, and we climb up to the cloud.

The days go by, and I can't stop thinking about my flower. I miss it terribly. I can't eat, I can't sleep. I love that flower.

Billy is upset... He asks what he can do for me. And suddenly, from one of his antlers, a little bud appear The bud opens...

...into a flower!

And Billy says:
- This flower is perhaps not as beautiful as your flower, but I offer it to you with all my heart.
- I didn't know that reindeer could grow flowers from their antlers, I said, amazed.
- I am not just any old reindeer, Pops, replies Billy, smiling. I am a flying reindeer.

And, I am your favourite reindeer.

JULY

m 1
t 2
w 3
t 4
f 5
S 6
S 7

Holiday!

m 8
t 9
w 10
t 11
f 12
S 13
S 14

Holiday schedule:

Have a snooze.

m 15
t 16
w 17
t 18
f 19
S 20
S 21

Write to
Snow White.

m 22
t 23
w 24
t 25
f 26
S 27
S 28

m 29
t 30
w 31

Have another snooze.

Shape my cloud
into a boat.

Notes from July

The summer holiday starts.

The elves go on their round-the-world trip; the reindeer, B
Thorwald and Linus, go to visit their cousins in Norway.

Billy stays with me. We decide to go to Earth for a
beach holiday.

We look for an island, but over the Atlantic Ocean we have a little problem: our cloud turns into rain, and Billy and I...

fall into the sea.

We swim for days and days.

Then one fine morning, we spy dry land.

continued in August..

AUGUST

t 1
f 2
S 3
S 4

m 5 Keep an eye on the crabs.

t 6

w 7 Remember to send
t 8 postcard to my
f 9 friend Little Mouse.
S 10
S 11

m 12
t 13
w 14 Check out the
t 15 hiding places for
f 16 my toys.
S 17
S 18

m 19 shooting stars.
t 20 (Open the umbrella
w 21 just in case.)
t 22
f 23
S 24
S 25

m 26 Find some
t 27 bananas.
w 28
t 29
f 30
S 31

Notes from August

continued
from July...

After swimming for a very long time in the ocean, we arrive at a beach bordered with palm trees.
- This place looks perfect for our holidays, I say.
- Oh perfectly perfect, adds Billy.

I put up the sun umbrella. Billy puts on his sunglasse then, suddenly, we hear a noise behind the palm trees.

And out pops a pretty little antelope.
Billy's eyes open wide and he goes to greet her:
– Hello! he says, wiggling his antlers. My name is Billy,
and this is my friend Pops. We are on holiday.
The antelope smiles. She and Billy go for a walk.

I am left stranded
on the beach, alone.

And now the crabs decide to jump out of the water. Fat lot of good it does me telling them that I am Father Christmas. They pinch me on the bott and find it very funny.

After several days of battling with the crabs, I go a look for Billy. When I find him, he is kissing the antelope.

When he finally stops kissing, I say to him:
- Excuse me for disturbing you, Billy, but it's time to get ba to our cloud.

My reindeer looks at me strangely. He is embarrassed.
- Pops, he says, I think I will stay on Earth. I am in love.

I'm very sad. I have known Billy for ever, and he has always been my favourite reindeer... But I understand. I hug Billy, I hug his beloved antelope...

...and I wait for a passing cloud to get me back home.

SEPTEMBER

S 1

m 2

t 3

w 4

t 5 Stuff and re-paint the cloud.

f 6 Lunch with Superman and Snow White.

S 7

S 8

m 9 Billy's birthday.

t 10

w 11

t 12 Elf school starts.

m 16

t 17

w 18

t 19

f 20

S 21

S 22 Autumn!

m 23

t 24

w 25

t 26

f 27 Begin making toys for Christmas.

S 28

S 29

Back to school: give elves a good combing.

Notes from September

Christmas is coming, so I start to make my toys. One evening, while I'm just finishing a huge soft bear, I burst into tears.

- What's the matter, Father Christmas? asks the bear, surprised.
- Sniff, I have been sad ever since my reindeer Billy left. I miss him so much.

Sniff sniff...

I cannot stop crying.

The toys, the elves, and the reindeer all open their
eyes in amazement. It's the first time they have seen me cr

– Father Christmas, says the bear, squeezing me tight,
I love you very much, I hate to see you so sad.

– We love you too! cry the elves.

– Us too! the reindeer shout.

Everyone comes to hug me. I feel as if I might suffocate...

...but at least I am not sad any more!

OCTOBER

t 1
w 2
t 3
f 4
S 5
S 6

Shape my cloud into a frying pan.

m 7 — Visit the dentist.
t 8
w 9
t 10 — Elf school.
f 11
S 12

m 14 — Do the housework.
t 15
w 16
t 17 — Sort out my socks.
f 18
S 19
S 20

m 21
t 22
w 23 — Pizza night.
t 24
f 25 — Finish making my Christmas toys.
S 26
S 27

Knitting lessons – so my legs are always warm!

Notes from October

I have nearly finished making my toys for Christmas. All I need now is some furry antelopes.

I try to make one, but she is completely hopeless. She frowns at me. She is not happy.

- I don't know how to make antelopes, I say.
- Try a bit harder, she replies.
    I sigh.
- I'm going to write to all the children who have asked for antelopes and tell them that there aren't any this year!
- But that's a lie! gasps the antelope. It's just that you can't be bothered to make antelopes, since your reindeer Billy went off to live with one on Earth. You are cross with all of us, even though we are very sweet creatures.

It was my turn to
frown at the antelope.

– How do you know that
Billy has gone to live
with an antelope?

– I know everything. Furry animals
always know everything.
I grumble a bit, but try again.
This time, she looks perfect.

So perfect, that
I make a whole herd.

NOVEMBER

f 1 — Shape my cloud into an envelope.

S 2

S 3

m 4

t 5

w 6

t 7

f 8

S 9

S 10

Read and file the first letters.

m 11 — Think about presents for the reindeer.

t 12

w 13 — Elf school.

m 18

t 19

w 20 — Make the very last presents.

t 21

f 22

S 23 — Get the sleigh ready.

S 24

m 25

t 26

w 27 — Sew the pockets on my red coat.

t 28

f 29

S 30

Gift-wrapping lesson.

Notes from November

Christmas is nearly here. I am sitting on my cloud and happily reading through my letters from children. The wind blows suddenly

and all the letters fly away!

I get my butterfly net, jump on Thorwald, my second favourite flying reindeer, and zoom after the letters. I catch one, two, three, ten, one hundred...

But there is still one cheeky little letter which swoops about all over the place.

I call out:

- Come here immediately!

But the letter flies up, up into the sky. It loops and twists and turns... I wonder what on earth could be written in such a cheeky letter.

I nearly fall off my reindeer trying to catch it. But, finally, I have the letter in my hands!

I take it out of the envelope, unfold it, and I read:

Dear
Father Christmas
Please could
I have a little
kite which flies
very high.
Gabriel
Age 5

That explains everything...

DECEMBER

S 1

m 2
t 3
w 4
t 5
f 6
S 7
S 8

File the letters.

m 9
t 10
w 11
t 12

Go and fetch the toys from my hiding places.

Elf school.

m 16
t 17
w 18
t 19
f 20
S 21
S 22

Start filling the sleigh with toys.

Check the sleigh one last time.

m 23
t 24
w 25
t 26
f 27
S 28
S 29

Deliver presents to the children.

Lesson in decorating Christmas tree: easy!

Shape cloud into a parcel.

Notes from December

Tonight it's Christmas Eve. My sleigh is overflowing with toys. I am ready to go and deliver the presents. The elves wave their handkerchiefs and shout:
– Goodbye, Father Christmas! Safe journey!

The reindeer, Bo, Linus and Thorwald are ready for take-off. I give them the signal...
but they don't move, not even a millimetre.

I open my eyes wide and ask them:
– What's going on?

– The sleigh is too heavy, there are too many toys, explains Thorwald. We can't take off!

Disaster! I'm getting hot and bothered in my red suit.
- Take out the presents for the least well-behaved children,
suggests Thorwald. We can deliver them another day.

I reply:
- We can't do that: it's Christmas Eve, and on this day,
even the most terrible little tykes and pesky pests have a
right to get their presents.

Time passes. I am still on my cloud, when I should be
stuffing presents into Christmas stockings. The children will
be so upset!

Suddenly, I see five black dots in the sky. They seem to be heading for us. Angry children are coming to find out what's happening! I get down from the sleigh and hide behind the reindeer. Then I hear shouts. Shouts of joy!

- Billy's back!
cry the elves.

Billy's back!

Billy's back!

I pull myself together. Billy, my favourite reindeer, who stayed on Earth with an antelope, is here with his wife and their three children. Overcome with joy, I run to kiss them. Then I attach them to the sleigh, and once again I give the signal for take-off,

and hop, off we go!!!

ACKNOWLEDGEMENTS

Thank you to all the elves who helped me to illustrate my story.

Elf Benjamin : pages 10 - 13, 20-21, 28-29, 34 - 37, 42-43, 52, 56 - 63, 72 - 75, 80 - 83 and 94-95.

Elf Aurélie : pages 22 to 27 and 53 to 55.

Elf Vanessa : pages 14-15, 30 - 32 and 48-49.

Elf Olivier : pages 6 to 9, 38 to 41, 76 to79 and 84 to 89.

Elf Christophe : pages 16 to 19, 50-51 and 92-93.

Elf Clément : pages 44 to 47 and 64 to 71.

Elf Miguel : bottom of diary pages.

my projects

For next year...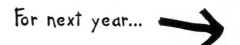

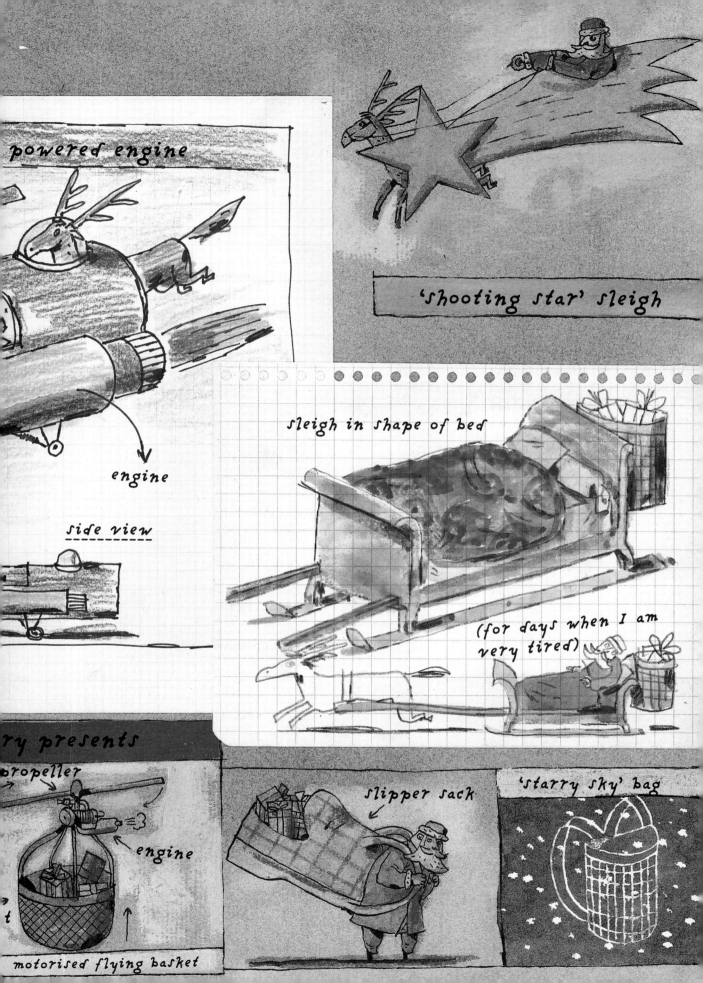

powered engine

'shooting star' sleigh

engine

side view

sleigh in shape of bed

(for days when I am very tired)

...ry presents

propeller

engine

motorised flying basket

slipper sack

'starry sky' bag

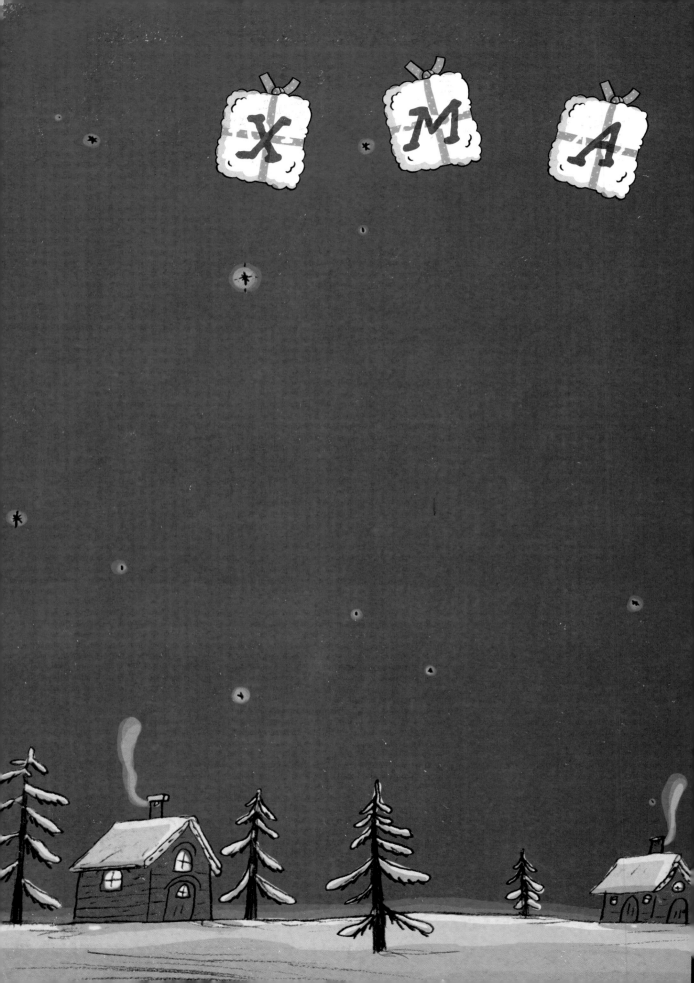